LITTLE EAGLE LEARNS TO FLY

Written by S. A. Cornell
Illustrated by John Jones

Troll Associates

Library of Congress Cataloging in Publication Data

Cornell, S.A.
   Little Eagle learns to fly.

   Summary: Elmo, a young eagle, has trouble learning
to fly but discovers that he is good at something else.
   [1. Eagles—Fiction. 2. Flight—Fiction. 3. Self-
acceptance—Fiction] I. Jones, John, 1935-   ill.
II. Title.
PZ7.C81635Li   1986   [E]   85-14086
ISBN 0-8167-0618-2 (lib. bdg.)
ISBN 0-8167-0619-0 (pbk.)

LITTLE EAGLE
LEARNS TO FLY

Max and Elmo Eagle were
brothers. They lived with their
parents on a sharp cliff at the
top of a mountain.

When Max and Elmo were very
small, they watched their
parents fly. They watched them
flap their great wings. They saw
them glide. They saw them soar.
Sometimes they saw them fly
above the clouds.

"I can't wait until we can fly, too," said Max.
"Me either," Elmo agreed.

Finally, the day came. Elmo
and Max were big enough to fly.
They stood at the edge of the
nest. They watched. Their
mother took off first. She moved
her wings smoothly to catch a
stream of air. She seemed to
float on the air. Then she
disappeared behind a cloud.

8

"Ah," said their father. "Your mother always was a beautiful flier. You will be, too."
A breeze rustled the nest as he showed his sons how to move their wings. Then he was off.

Elmo and Max stood at the edge of the nest. They looked down the cliffs.

Elmo looked over the peaks. He already knew a lot about the mountains. He knew that the weather could change in a minute. A storm could race in faster than an eagle could fly.

Elmo watched Max perch his
toes over the nest.
"See you in the air," called Max,
as he took off.

Elmo watched his brother. Max dropped straight down at first. Then he began to move his broad wings. Slowly, Max lifted up with the wind.
Max circled right. He circled left. He flew low. He poked above the clouds. He joined his parents. And the three of them traced smooth shapes in the air.

Elmo felt stuck at the edge of
the nest. He couldn't let go.
"I must try," said Elmo. "After
all, I *am* an eagle."

His knees shook. *Swoosh!* A gust
of wind swept him away.

But something was wrong. Elmo
felt all tangled. He didn't know
if his wings were up or down.
He couldn't see where he was
going.
"I don't think this is right,"
thought Elmo as he tumbled
through the air. "I don't think
this is flying."

Bamm! Elmo fell onto a thick branch that stuck out from a rock. He was lucky. He had hurt only his feelings. His parents had seen him fall and they helped him home.

Safe in the nest, the family
discussed Elmo's first flight.

"I don't think he flaps enough,"
said his mother.
"I don't think he glides on the
wind," said his father.
"I don't think he looks where he
is going," said Max.

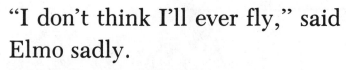

"I don't think I'll ever fly," said
Elmo sadly.
"Nonsense!" said his father.

But Elmo's parents were really
very upset.
"Maybe something went wrong
before he was hatched," said his
mother. "Maybe we didn't sit
softly enough on his egg."

"Maybe we should have helped
him crack the shell," said his
father.

News spread quickly. Soon all
the eagles knew about Elmo, the
terrible flier. Everyone had
ideas about how to help him.

"Have him do warm-up exercises," suggested Uncle Ralph.

"Make sure he eats a light breakfast," warned Aunt Kate.

"Clip his toenails," warned Cousin Matilda. "They're too long."

They tried everything. But Elmo
was still a terrible flier.

"Don't worry," said his mother.
"Some eagles learn things later
than others. You'll be fine."
Elmo wanted to believe her. He
hoped she was right. All in all,
he felt awful.

Soon Max was taking lessons at
a school for super-fliers. In no
time he could dive. He could
soar. He could do triple loop-
dee-doos with one eye shut.

Elmo practiced every day. But
he didn't get far.
"Just follow me," Max offered.
But nothing worked for Elmo.

One day Elmo's family went out flying together. Elmo stayed home and felt sorry for himself.

"It's no fun being an eagle who can't fly," he said to himself. "But there must be things that I *can* do well. Of course, I know how to play well with Max. I can also keep a neat nest."

Elmo thought hard and made a
wonderful discovery. Sitting
quietly in the nest, Elmo found
he could hear even the tiniest
sound.

"I may be a terrible flier," he
said. "But I'm a great listener!"

Elmo could hear eagles take off
from the rocky cliffs. He could
hear ants building sandy hills in
the rocks. He could hear wisps
of clouds tearing apart. In fact,
Elmo could hear better than any
eagle who ever lived.

Now he felt much better about
himself.
"I'm good at something, too,"
he said happily.

He sat on the edge of the nest.
He listened carefully. He heard
the sounds of the valley below.

He heard the cows moo. He
heard the sheep baa. He heard
the river splash.

He heard the sounds of the
mountains. Wind whistled past
the rocks. Water trickled down
the mountain. Little stones
clinked against bigger ones.

He listened to the sky. Wings
rustled in the air. Clouds swept
overhead. Leaves fluttered high
like sails in the breeze.

Then Elmo heard a low,
rumbling sound in the sky. Most
eagles wouldn't have heard it.
But Elmo knew what it was
right away.

"Rolling thunder!" he said.
"Thunder that growls as it rolls
in from the sea. A storm is
coming in fast. A storm that can
race faster than an eagle can
fly."

Elmo was glad to be safe in the
nest. Then he remembered his
family. They were out flying
while a storm was racing in!

"What should I do?" he asked.
"What *can* I do? A good flier
would go out and get his family.
But I'm Elmo, the terrible
flier."

The thunder rumbled again.
Elmo was scared. But he knew
what he had to do. He took a
deep breath. Then he jumped
from the nest.

At first he tumbled around in
the air. He spun. He bounced.
He fell. Then he caught the
wind. He thought of his family.
And Elmo, the terrible flier,
flew.

He flew and he listened. He
listened for the rustle of his
family's wings. But he heard
only the rolling thunder. It was
getting closer. It began to crash
around him. But still, Elmo
flew.

He flew through wide open
spaces. He flew past narrow
cliffs. He flew as raindrops
began to fall. As he flew, he
listened. Then finally, he heard
them.

"Look, it's Elmo!" shouted his
mother.
"Look how well he's flying!"
said his father.
"Even in the raindrops," added
Max.

"It's not just raindrops," shouted
Elmo. "It's a huge storm. I
heard rolling thunder. Follow
me. We'll race the storm."

Elmo used his great hearing to
fly home around the storm. In
the nest, his mother hugged
him. Then his father hugged
him. Then Max hugged him.

"You saved us, Elmo," they
said.
Elmo felt wonderful.
"I'm still Elmo," he said. "But
I'm not Elmo, the terrible flier
anymore."

46

"Each eagle learns in a different way—and at a different time," said Elmo's mother. "I knew you'd be fine in the end."

And she was right. Every eagle on the cliffs agreed. Now they called him Elmo, the brave flier of the rolling thunder!